Beautiful You, Beautiful Me

Tasha Spillett-Sumner

Illustrated by

Salini Perera

Owlkids Books

For my mother, who reminds us
that we belong deeply to one another —*T.S.*

For Naiomi —*S.P.*

Beautiful You,
Beautiful Me

Izzy loves her mama's hugs.

Wrapped tight in Mama's arms
is Izzy's favorite place to be.

Skin to skin.

Safe and warm.

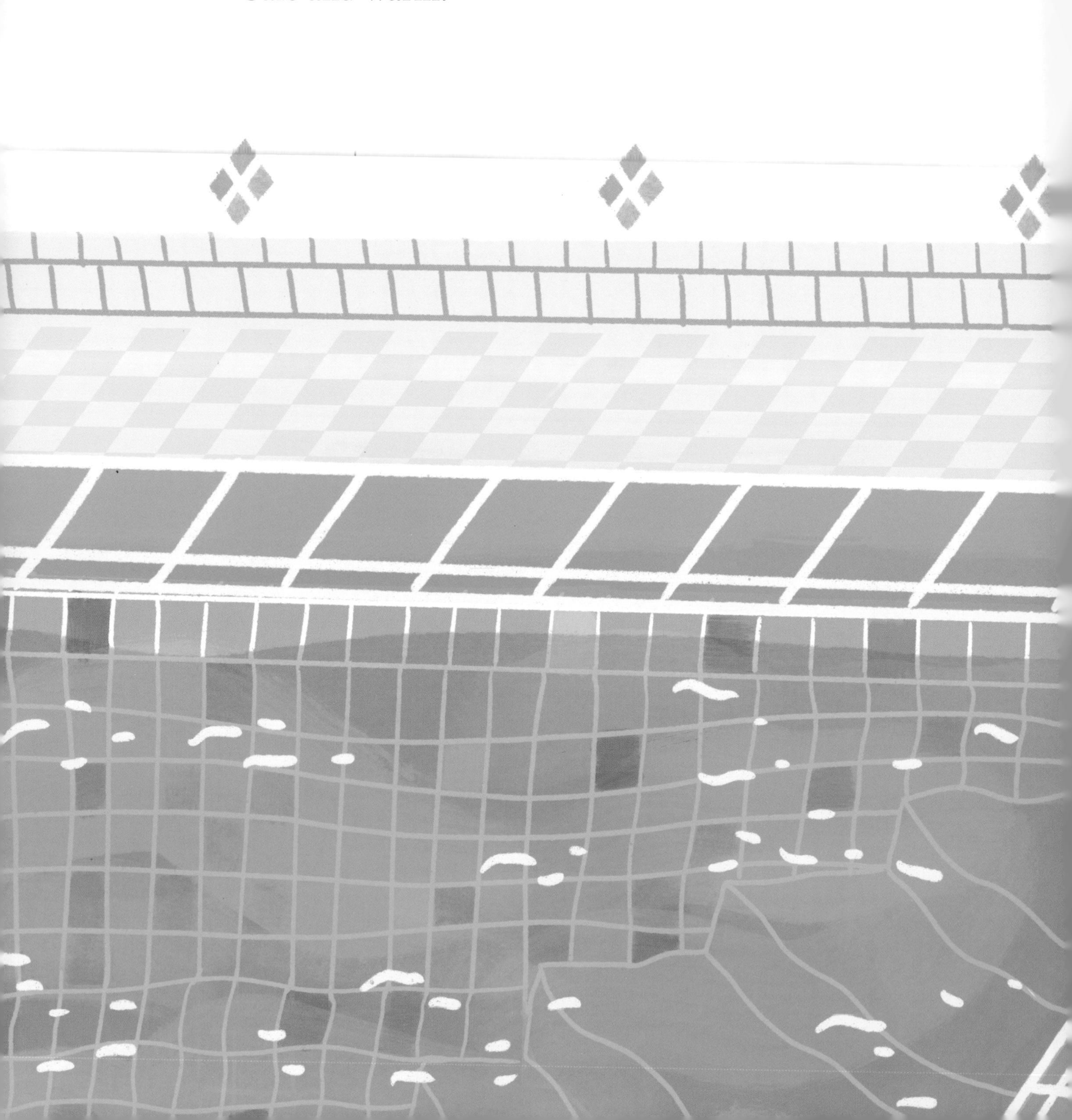

One night, wrapped tight in Mama's arms, Izzy noticed something she had never noticed before.

Mama's hug felt the same.

Safe and warm as ever.

But Izzy saw that her skin and Mama's skin looked different.

“Mama!” exclaimed Izzy. “We don’t match! You’re sand, and I’m chocolate.”

Izzy wasn’t sure how she felt about not matching Mama.

When Izzy looked at Mama, she saw only beautiful things, and she wanted to be just the same.

But Mama pulled Izzy close.

You're part of me,
and I'm part of you.

I'm beautiful like me,
and you're beautiful like you.

The next morning, while Mama was braiding her hair, Izzy noticed that her hair and Mama's hair were different too.

Izzy's hair had big swirls and curls that jumped out from her braids.

Mama's hair was smooth and straight, and her braid hung right down the middle of her back.

When they danced, Izzy's hair grew bigger and bigger, while Mama's hair swayed side to side like a happy puppy's tail.

"Mama!" exclaimed Izzy. "Our hair doesn't match! Yours is straight, and mine is curly."

But Mama lovingly twirled her
finger in one of Izzy's curls.

You're part of me,
and I'm part of you.

I'm beautiful like me,
and you're beautiful like you.

Izzy wanted her hair to sway side to side like a happy puppy's tail too, but her curls kept springing up!

Why couldn't she look more like Mama? Izzy wanted to be *Mama's* kind of beautiful.

That afternoon, Mama took Izzy for a walk.

They saw a mama duck teaching her ducklings to swim.

They saw a mama cat cleaning her kittens.

They saw a mama bird
feeding her nestlings.

“Mama!” exclaimed Izzy. “Not all mamas and babies match.”

“But they still belong to one another,” added Mama.

At bedtime, Mama looked into Izzy's big, bright eyes.

"Izzy!" she exclaimed. "Our eyes don't match! Yours are earth, and mine are water."

Izzy gave Mama a big hug.

I'm part of you,
and you're part of me.

I'm beautiful like me,
and you're beautiful like you.

Izzy snuggled into Mama's arms and fell asleep.

Safe and warm in her favorite place to be.

Owlkids Books acknowledges the financial support of the Canada Council for the Arts, the Ontario Arts Council, the Government of Canada through the Canada Book Fund (CBF) and the Government of Ontario through the Ontario Creates Book Initiative for our publishing activities.

Published in Canada by
Owlkids Books Inc.
1 Eglinton Avenue East
Toronto, ON M4P 3A1

Published in the United States by
Owlkids Books Inc.
1700 Fourth Street
Berkeley, CA 94710

Library and Archives Canada Cataloguing in Publication

Title: Beautiful you, beautiful me / by Tasha Spillett-Sumner ; illustrated by Salini Perera.
Names: Spillett-Sumner, Tasha, 1988- author. | Perera, Salini, 1986- illustrator.
Identifiers: Canadiana 20210390298 | ISBN 9781771474528 (hardcover)
Classification: LCC PS8637.P55 B43 2022 | DDC jC813/.6—dc23

Library of Congress Control Number: 2021951816

Edited by Jennifer Stokes
Designed by Claudia Dávila

Manufactured in Guangdong Province, Dongguan City, China, in March 2022,
by Toppan Leefung Packaging & Printing (Dongguan) Co., Ltd.
Job #BAYDC106

A B C D E F

MIX
Paper from responsible sources
FSC® C104723

Canada Council for the Arts
Conseil des Arts du Canada

Canada

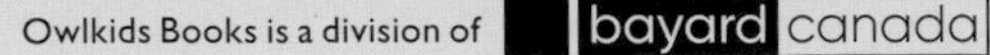